# Go, Gina!

By Julie Bryant

Illustrated by Warwick Bennett

# Chapter 1

# *Before the Race*

It was race day at last.
Gina was feeling very excited.
She had arrived at the BMX track
early with her parents.

Every day for three weeks,
Gina had come down to the track
with her dad to practice.
Now she was ready for her first race.

"Hi!" Gina called to Carlos and two other children.
"This is going to be great fun.
I can hardly wait for our race!"

"The track looks good," said Carlos.
"I have just checked it out.
We'll have to be careful on the whoop-de-doos.
They could be slippery!"

Soon it was their turn.
They pushed their bikes over to the starting gate.

# Chapter 2

# A Flying Start

"Are you ready, riders?" called the man
with the microphone.

Gina stood up high on her bike.
She really wanted to do her best.

As the starting gate dropped with a crash,
Gina pushed down hard on the pedals.
The four riders were off to a flying start.
Down the ramp they raced and onto the track.

The riders were still in one line
until they got to the first turn.
Around they went, riding up the bank,
then back down again onto the track.

All the people watching were shouting and waving,
"Come on! Come on! You can do it!"

Carlos was pedaling very hard now,
and little by little,
he began to move ahead of the others.

Faster and faster he pedaled,
but Gina was riding hard, too,
and she began to close in on him.

Carlos knew he had to keep up his speed
because Gina was so close behind him.
He didn't want her to pass him.
The biggest jump was just in front of them.

Everyone was shouting louder than ever,
**"Go, Gina! Go, Carlos!"**

Over the jump they went and down they came,
their back wheels hitting the track
almost at the same time.

Gina could hear the people shouting,
but she didn't turn her head to look at them.
If her bike wobbled, she could fall off.

# Chapter 3

# *The Big Crash*

The four riders bent down
as they rode over the bumps.
Carlos was still in the lead,
and Gina was not far behind him.

People were jumping up and down,
shouting and waving to them.

Carlos was going to win.
He just had to go over the whoop-de-doos,
around the last turn,
and then down to the finish line.

Suddenly he skidded in some wet mud
and came off his bike.

Carlos wasn't hurt,
but his bike had slid right across the track
in front of Gina.
She knew that she couldn't stop in time.

Gina was thinking quickly.
If she went to the left,
the other two riders would crash into her.
If she went to the right, she could hit Carlos.
There was only one thing that she could do.
She lifted her front wheel high
and jumped over his bike.

14

Now Gina was in the lead.
She kept pedaling very fast
over the whoop-de-doos
and down to the finish line.
Gina had won!

"What a great race!" shouted her dad
as he ran to meet her.

"Yes!" laughed Gina.
"That was so much fun!"